A long time ago in Japan, there lived two frogs. One of the frogs lived in a ditch close to the beach. He liked his home, and would often go for a paddle in the sea. But he longed to see the rest of Japan. He had heard that there were big lakes, old temples, and cherry blossom trees.

"One day I will see all of these things," he said to himself.

The other frog lived far away by a stream that ran between a lake and an old temple. She was fond of her home, too. She liked to sit by the trickling stream and look at the fish. But she longed to explore as well.

"If only I could see the sea," she said to herself.

So one morning, the two frogs packed their bags and set off. They did not know it, but each of them lived at opposite ends of the same long road. As they hopped along the road, each frog hopped closer to the other.

At first, the frogs enjoyed their journey. They said a friendly good morning to everyone they came across.

"Good morning, Bird," said the beach-side frog.

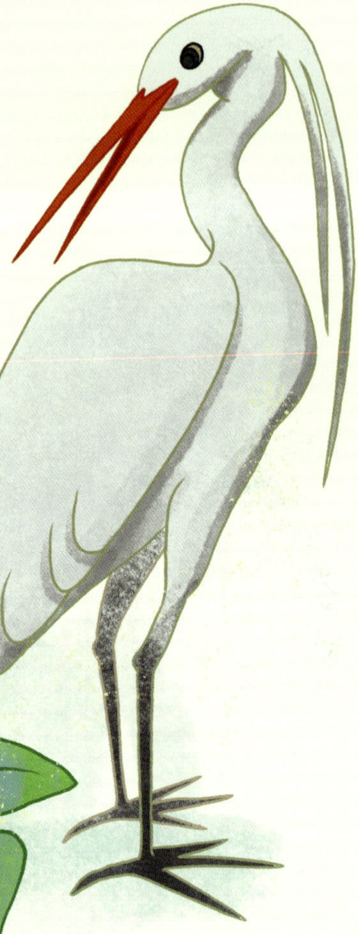

"Good morning, Snail," said the stream-side frog.

But the journey was long, and the day was hot. Then, midway along the road, there was a tall mountain. To go around the mountain would take too long, so the two frogs had to hop over it.

The two frogs hopped and hopped, but they were still far from the top. As the day got hotter, the frogs got more and more tired. Around midday, they each stopped in a cool, damp spot for a while to catch their breath.

As they rested, the two frogs looked back at where they had come from. The beach-side frog looked back at the sea, with the sunlight twinkling on it. At the same time, the stream-side frog looked back at her stream, glinting in the sunshine.

“I hope the lakes and temples will be as marvelous as the sea,” said the beach-side frog to himself.

On the other side of the mountain, the stream-side frog said, “I hope the sea will be as dazzling as my stream.”

Now rested, the frogs hopped on. Up and up they went. They hopped around trees, and alongside parks and rivers.

Much hopping later, the two frogs reached the top of the mountain. When they got there, they were surprised to see each other!

"Well, goodness me," the beach-side frog said, "another frog!"

"Well, I never," said the stream-side frog, "another frog!"

The two frogs told each other about their homes and their wish to explore.

“What a pity that we are not taller, because then we could see where we want to go from the top of this mountain,” said the stream-side frog.

“I know,” said the beach-side frog, “we can stand up on our back legs, and hold onto each other. That will make us taller.”

So the two frogs stretched up and leaned against each other. The beach-side frog pointed his nose at the lakes, and the stream-side frog pointed her nose at the sea.

However, the two frogs forgot that when they were upright with their noses pointing forwards, they were in fact looking back at where they had come from!

"Well, goodness me!" said the beach-side frog. "There is no point in carrying on with this long journey. The lakes look exactly the same as the sea!"

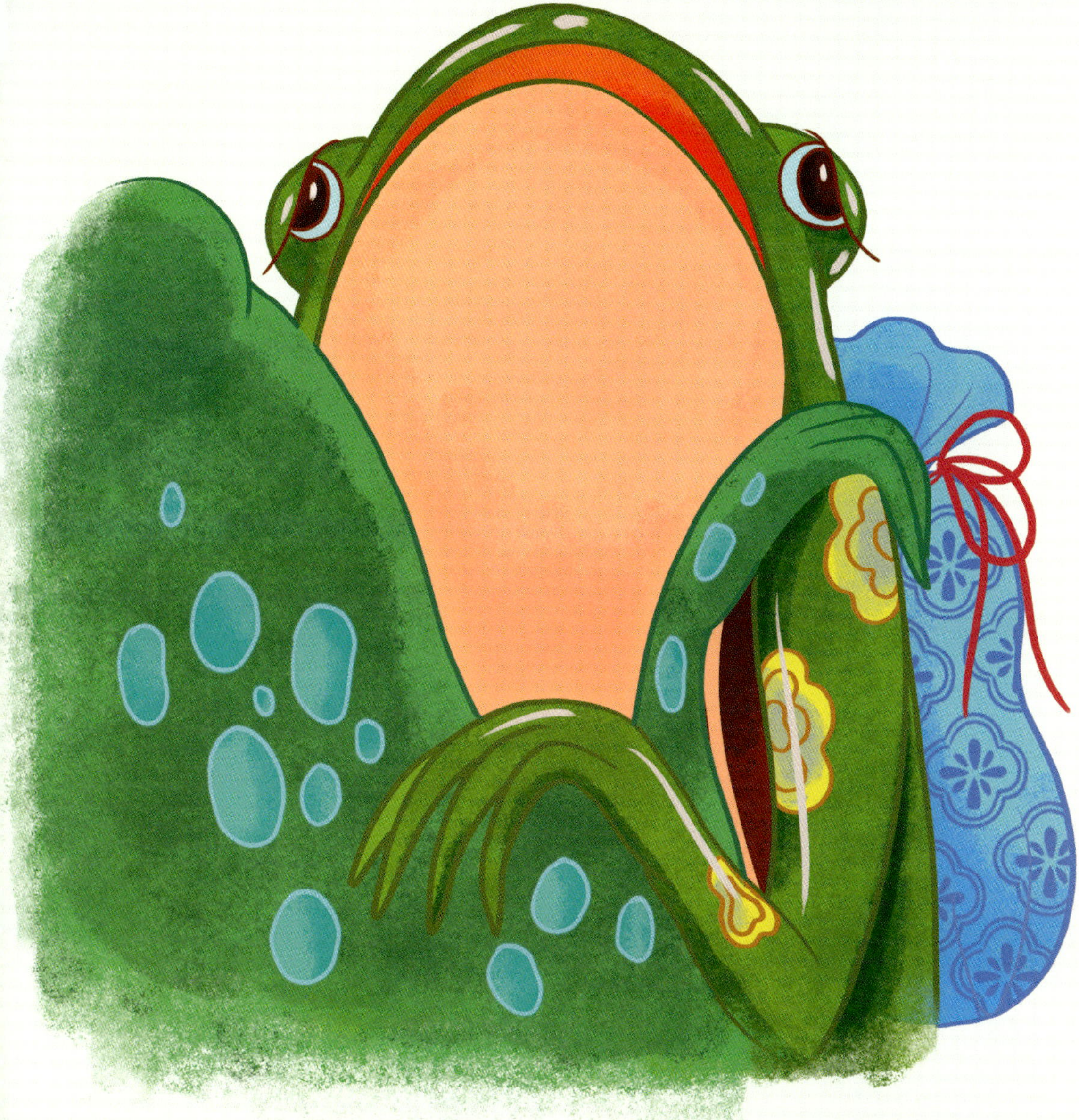

"Well, I never!" said the stream-side frog. "The sea is much smaller than I have been told. In fact, it is no bigger than a lake! If I had known that before setting off, I would never have traveled this far."

With that, the two frogs let go of each other and flopped to the ground. They said goodbye to each other and set off for home, never to understand their mistake.